W9-DGP-395

Duncan and the Pirates

written and illustrated by
Peter Utton

PICTURE WINDOW BOOKS
Minneapolis, Minnesota

Managing Editor: Catherine Neitge
Story Consultant: Terry Flaherty
Page Production: Melissa Kes
Creative Director: Keith Griffin
Editorial Director: Carol Jones

First American edition published in 2006 by
Picture Window Books
5115 Excelsior Boulevard
Suite 232
Minneapolis, MN 55416
1-877-845-8392
www.picturewindowbooks.com

First published in Great Britain by
A & C Black Publishers Limited
37 Soho Square, London W1D 3QZ
Text and illustrations copyright © 2003 Peter Utton

Library of Congress Cataloging-in-Publication Data
Utton, Peter.
Duncan and the pirates / written and illustrated by Peter Utton.
p. cm. — (Read-it! chapter books)
Summary: The fierce and retired pirate Mr. Hipstone and his soppy dog Duncan try
to stop Captain Bootleg from stealing their buried treasure.
ISBN 1-4048-1277-6 (hard cover)
[1. Pirates—Fiction. 2. Dogs—Fiction. 3. Buried treasure—Fiction.] I. Title. II. Series.
PZ7.U73Dun 2005
[E]—dc22   2005007187

Table of Contents

Chapter One

Duncan is a sweet dog. He looks sweet,

acts sweet,

and thinks sweet thoughts.

Duncan lives with a fierce, old grump
called Mr. Hipstone.

Mr. Hipstone
looks fierce,

acts fierce,

and probably thinks fierce
(and grumpy) thoughts.

Duncan and Mr. Hipstone have been together for a long time. When you see Duncan, you know that Mr. Hipstone is not far away.

And when you see
Mr. Hipstone,
you know
Duncan
is close by.

Some people think Mr. Hipstone was
something big in the city.

Some people think he's a retired pirate.

But nobody has ever asked him because
he looks so fierce.

Sometimes Mr. Hipstone is forgetful. Last Thursday, he forgot to buy any supper ...

and he couldn't find any money to buy food. He looked in his city suit.

He looked in his big
pirate pockets.
Nothing.
All empty.

Mr. Hipstone looked down at Duncan and
said "Aaargh!" in a fierce and growly
voice. Duncan's tail wagged. He knew
exactly what Mr. Hipstone meant.

Chapter Two

That night, Duncan and Mr. Hipstone
went down to the river, climbed aboard
their ship, and sailed out of town.

Just as the sun was coming up, they
reached a secret island. They dropped the
anchor and rowed ashore.

Mr. Hipstone looked fiercely along the beach and into the forest. He looked down at Duncan. "Arrgh!" he growled.

Sniffing and snuffling, Duncan set off at a brisk pace. After a while, he stopped and sniffed into the sand.

Mr. Hipstone's fierce little eyes lit up.
"Arrgh!" he growled.

Duncan looked up at Mr. Hipstone with
a sandy nose, huffed loudly,
shook his head, and ...

trotted off again, nose to the ground.

An hour later, after much snuffling and huffing, Duncan stopped. He sniffed and snuffled, and his tail wagged furiously. He dug his paws into the sand and started digging like a mad thing.

Mr. Hipstone disappeared under a shower of sand.
"Arrgh!" he croaked.

Mr. Hipstone started digging fiercely.
Duncan disappeared under a shower of sand.

Mr. Hipstone dug deeper and deeper.

Duncan sat and watched. He yawned.

He was just settling down for a little
doze, when ...

Mr. Hipstone's spade hit something solid.
"Arrgh!" he shouted.
"Mmmm!" thought Duncan, and he
licked his chops.

A moment later, Mr. Hipstone held up not
a treasure chest, but a huge juicy bone.
"Arrgh!" he growled, and threw the bone
in the air.

Duncan's tail wagged wildly.

"ARRGH!" roared Mr. Hipstone, and he grabbed at the bone, but Duncan rushed off with it, tail whirling.

"ARRGH!" roared Mr. Hipstone again. Duncan stopped and looked back.

Chapter Three

Duncan dashed back and peered into
the hole.

"Arrgh!" growled Mr. Hipstone.
Duncan sniffed suspiciously.

With Mr. Hipstone holding the other end of the bone, Duncan slowly hauled him out.

As Duncan sat back, puffing and panting, Mr. Hipstone snatched up the bone and raced off, shouting "ARRGH!"

Suddenly, Mr. Hipstone heard a pitiful
doggy cry. He stopped and looked back.

whoo-oooO!

Duncan lay on the sand with his feet in
the air.

"Arrgh!" muttered Mr. Hipstone,
and hurried back
down the hill.

Mr. Hipstone looked at
Duncan very closely.

Duncan opened one eye, whined, and
licked Mr. Hipstone's nose. "Arrgh!"
growled Mr. Hipstone.

Duncan opened his other eye ...

leapt to his feet, grabbed the bone,
and was off again, tail twirling madly.

"ARRGH!" roared Mr. Hipstone.

Mr. Hipstone followed Duncan's doggy
footprints to the side of a sandy hill.

Huge showers of sand were being flung
into the air.

A moment later, he saw a wonderful sight. "Arrgh!" he growled.

Duncan huffed the sand from his nose, sat back, and scratched his ear.
Mr. Hipstone unlocked his treasure chest and was just about to say, "Arrgh!" ...

when a cannonball split the palm tree
above his head.

Duncan and Mr. Hipstone crept to the top of the hill.

"Arrgh!" growled Mr. Hipstone.

Duncan sniffed the breeze and recognized their old enemy, Captain Rottenleg and his horrible crew. Duncan's sweet hackles rose. He growled and rushed toward the beach.

"Arrgh!" shouted Mr. Hipstone.
But Duncan was gone.

Chapter Four

Captain Rottenleg grinned at his horrible crew. "That's Cap'n Hipstone's ship, right enough mates, and where he be, so be his treasure!"

A fierce, furry fireball rushed from the trees.

The horrible crew stared. Captain
Rottenleg glared at his horrible crew.
"What?" he snarled. "WHAT?"
He turned around just as ...

Duncan arrived in a fierce flurry of sand. He grabbed Captain Rottenleg by his wooden leg, and dragged him along the beach.

"Waaagh!" shouted Captain Rottenleg.
"What is it? Get it off me!"

The horrible crew charged after their captain and grabbed Duncan from all sides.

"I know you!" shouted Captain Rottenleg. "You be Cap'n Hipstone's dog! Tie him up, men!"

"Now, you scurvy hound,
we'll find out how much you're
worth to your beloved Captain Hipstone.
You can walk the plank, aha!"

Duncan edged out along the plank,
wishing he'd eaten the huge juicy bone
when he'd had the chance.

Mr. Hipstone stepped out from the trees.
"ARRGH!" he roared, and he held up the
treasure chest.

Captain Rottenleg glared at Mr. Hipstone.
"Well, Cap'n, you must be getting old.
Giving up your treasure for a dog!" He
poked Mr. Hipstone in the tummy with his
sword. "Getting fat, too! Ho! Ho! Ho!"

"I'll give you two minutes to get off the island," snarled Captain Rottenleg, "and take that mutt with you!"

Chapter Five

Mr. Hipstone rowed fiercely out to the ship, the pirates' jeers ringing in his ears. Duncan's head hung low. Mr. Hipstone had saved him, but it had cost them the treasure. No supper for them tonight!

Duncan couldn't look at Mr. Hipstone, so he looked back at the island instead.

He saw the horrible crew's jeers turn to
cries of rage when they broke open the
treasure chest. It was empty—except for
the huge juicy bone!

Suddenly, Duncan jumped to his feet,
turned, and looked at Mr. Hipstone's
big fat tummy.

"Arrgh!" growled Mr. Hipstone.

On board their ship, Mr. Hipstone unbuttoned his shirt. Duncan's tail wagged madly as hundreds of gold coins cascaded onto the deck.

Captain Rottenleg and his horrible crew
heard a distant "Arrgh!" as they
saw Duncan and Mr. Hipstone sailing
home to the biggest and the best supper
they'd ever had.

After supper, Duncan and Mr. Hipstone
sat by the fire and listened to the radio.
Duncan gazed up at Mr. Hipstone, and
Mr. Hipstone gazed fiercely down at Duncan.

Later, when Duncan was dozing,
Mr. Hipstone looked at his dog. He
reached out and scraggled Duncan's
sweet ears. Duncan's tail beat sleepily
on the fireside rug.

"Arrgh," growled Mr. Hipstone softly.

Most of the time, Duncan is a sweet dog. And most of the time, Mr. Hipstone is a fierce old grump.

But not all of the time!

About the author

Peter Utton has written and illustrated many books for children. His work has won numerous awards.

Look for More *Read-It!* Chapter Books

Bricks for Breakfast by Julia Donaldson

Hetty the Yeti by Dee Shulman

Spookball Champions by Scoular Anderson

The Mean Team from Mars by Scoular Anderson

Toby and His Old Tin Tub by Colin West

Looking for a specific title or level? A complete list of *Read-it!* Chapter Books is available on our Web site: **www.picturewindowbooks.com**